Roger's Umbrella

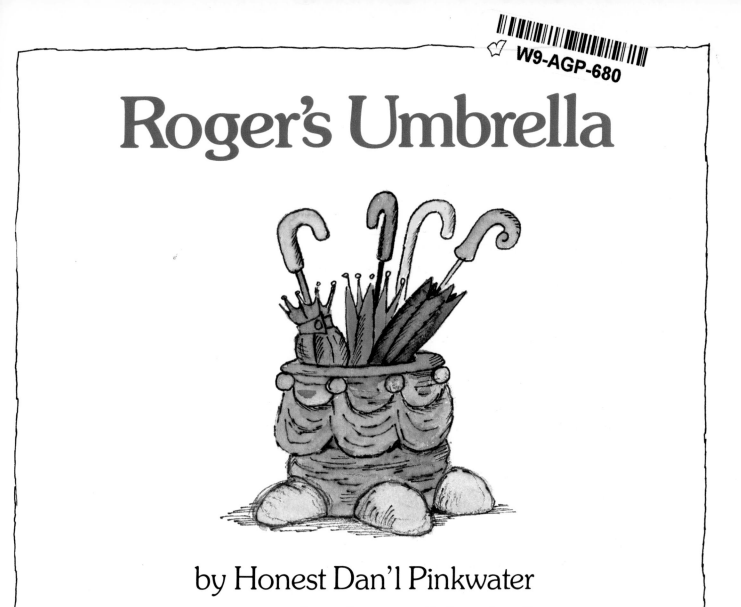

by Honest Dan'l Pinkwater
pictures by James Marshall

E. P. Dutton · New York

to Walter, a good friend, and cat

Text copyright © 1982 by Daniel M. Pinkwater
Illustrations copyright © 1982 by James Marshall

Unicorn is a registered trademark of E. P. Dutton.

Library of Congress number 81-2294
ISBN 0-525-44223-5

Published in the United States by E. P. Dutton
2 Park Avenue, New York, N.Y. 10016
a division of NAL Penguin Inc.

Published simultaneously in Canada by
Fitzhenry & Whiteside Limited, Toronto

Editor: Ann Durell   Designer: Riki Levinson

Printed in Hong Kong by South China Printing Co.
First Unicorn Edition 1985   COBE
10 9 8 7 6 5

When Roger left for school on rainy days, or days that looked like they might be rainy, his mother always said to him, "Roger, be sure to take your umbrella."

He didn't like taking his umbrella. For one thing, it got in the way. And for another, he didn't like the way the umbrella behaved.

Sometimes the umbrella would suddenly turn itself inside out for no reason.

Sometimes it would catch a gust of wind and make Roger walk on tiptoe.

It would suddenly pop open and hop around the room. It would flap like a big bird or bat. It would try to escape out the window.

Roger would have to grab the umbrella and struggle with it until he could finally stuff it into his closet, where it would thump and flap for hours.

THE ALAMO

He told his mother about it. He told her that he didn't like his umbrella, that it was a wild umbrella, and he wanted another one. "An umbrella is an umbrella," she said. "They're all the same."

Once, on a very windy day, Roger got picked up and blown almost a block in the wrong direction. It happened five times and he was late for school.

It seemed to Roger that the umbrella was getting worse and worse.

One night it almost escaped through the window. Roger managed to catch it by the handle, but the umbrella popped open. Roger couldn't pull it back in, so he just held on until the umbrella got tired. It took almost an hour.

Then the umbrella started to lift Roger high in the air whenever it got a chance. Sometimes it would lift him ten or fifteen feet and carry him for blocks and blocks.

People would shout, "Hey, come down from there! Don't you know that's dangerous?"

Roger was too busy hanging on and being scared to answer.

Sometimes the umbrella would put Roger down in places he did not know. He had to ask policemen how to get home.

And he would be late for supper.
When his mother complained,
Roger would tell her that it wasn't
his fault. It was the umbrella's fault.

"An umbrella is an umbrella,"
she would say. "They're all the
same."

One day, Roger was about to leave for school. It was very windy. "You'd better take your umbrella," his mother said. "It looks like rain." Roger took his umbrella.

He had hardly gone a
block when the umbrella
popped open, all by itself.

The wind picked up the
umbrella and Roger at once,
and blew them very high.

Higher than they'd ever been before. It blew them higher than the rooftops.

Roger hung on.

People and cars looked small beneath them.

"You awful umbrella," he said. "I hate you."

The umbrella seemed to stand still, high in the air. It rocked back and forth. Roger looked down. He didn't like it.

"Put me down, you stupid umbrella!" he shouted.

Slowly, the umbrella began to drift downward.
Roger had no idea where he was going.

At last the umbrella put him down inside a
high brick wall.

The umbrella started to flap. Roger tackled it and managed to wrestle it to the ground. Then he sat on it. Every now and then the umbrella twisted or struggled.

"Will you be still, you stupid umbrella?" Roger growled.

He saw three old ladies rushing out of a big house. Each of them was waving an umbrella. As they came closer, Roger could hear what they were saying.

"See, there he is. I saw him jump
right over the wall!"

"No, no, no! He fell from a tree!"

"I saw him having a fight with an
enormous black poodle dog."

"Excuse me," Roger said. "I didn't jump over the wall, and I didn't fall from a tree, and it wasn't a black poodle dog I was fighting with—it was my umbrella. It dropped me here. It's always doing things like that."

"Why that's shocking!" said one of the old ladies.
"Distressing!" said another.
"I believe it is against the law," said the third. "The very idea! Letting an umbrella run wild like that!"
"It's not my fault," Roger said. "Whoops, there it goes again!"

"So that's how it is," said an old lady.
"BLOOGIE! HORST! NAFFLE!"
Roger's umbrella folded itself and
came quietly to rest.

"You have to know how to talk to them. Now come inside and have some tea and cookies."

The inside of the big house was full of all sorts of odd things. Even the cookies were in the shape of lizards and shoes.

"Would you like us to teach you how to talk to your umbrella?" the old ladies asked Roger. Roger said he would like that very much.

"BLOOGIE! HOOP! DUP!" they shouted.
And all the umbrellas, including Roger's,
flew up and around the room.

"NAFFLE!" shouted the old ladies. And all the umbrellas furled themselves neatly and returned to their places.

"And that is how one talks to umbrellas," the old ladies told Roger.

Roger was delighted. He spent the whole day learning how to talk to his umbrella. Late in the afternoon, the old ladies took him back to the garden wall.

"Remember," they told him, "an umbrella is an umbrella—they're all the same."

Roger thanked them for the visit, and the tea and cookies, and the useful information.

Then he said to his umbrella, "BLOOGIE! HOOP! DWING!" And they floated over the wall, and over the housetops, and headed for home.